The Two Doors

by Shelly Forgey

Illustrations by Stephanie Doster

True Potential
REACH THE WORLD

THE TWO DOORS
Shelly Forgey
Illustrations by Stephanie Doster

ISBN: 978-1-935769-74-3 (hardcover)
ISBN: 978-1-935769-75-0 (eBook)

True Potential, Inc
PO Box 904
Travelers Rest, SC 29690
www.truepotentialmedia.com

Printed in the United States of America.

Gracie

The Bad Thing happened so long ago that Gracie could not remember how old she was then, although for a seven-year-old, such a detail seemed unimportant.

What was important was that shortly afterward, she and her whole family had moved to a new town, and Gracie had a very difficult time making new friends, for the Bad Person who had done the Bad Thing to her said, "No one will want to be friends with you." So she carried her sad story with her like a raggedy stuffed bear, and never spoke of it to any of her friends, and became very lonely.

Gracie's mother was sweet and loving. She took good care of Gracie and her little brother, but she was often tired and sad because Gracie's father left them the year before, and Gracie's mother worked too hard and too long each day, trying to make ends meet. How Gracie missed the long afternoon cuddles in the soft blue chair where her mother talked with her and sang silly songs to her. Now the afternoons were long but very lonely as Mrs. Carson from across the hall watched TV in Gracie's apartment until Gracie's mother returned from work. School would start next week, and maybe that would be better than staying home with no one but her little brother, Nicholas, and Mrs. Carson.

Gracie looked forward to bedtime because Mommy took a few minutes to stroke her face and sing her one very short song before kissing her good night. She left the door ajar and the night light on in the hallway because that was how Gracie and Nicky liked it. There was just enough of a glow to ward off the thick, inky black dark that they both hated, but not so much that it made their eyes jumpy so they couldn't fall asleep.

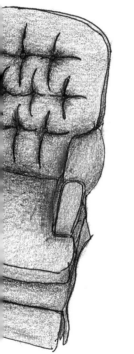

Tonight after Mommy's song, Gracie felt restless instead of sleepy. She began to remember the Bad Thing again, even though she didn't really like to, and she thought of her blankie in the back of her old toy box. Blankie had been there with her when she came home from the hospital as a newborn, Mommy had told her, and every day and night after that. She loved it so much that she cried whenever Mommy took it from her to wash, so Mommy began to sneak it into the washing machine while Gracie was playing with her dolls or watching TV. Blankie went along with her on every car ride and every trip to the park, and her blankie was with her when the Bad Thing happened. Since then, Gracie kept blankie tucked away because she could not bear to hold it, but she could not bear to part with it, either.

Silently, Gracie slid from the bed and crept to the toy box, sneaking a glance at Nicholas to make sure he was still asleep. As quiet as a mouse, quieter even, Gracie raised the lid and felt through the toys for the object she sought. At last, taking a very long time because we all know how long it takes to be quieter than a mouse, her hand touched

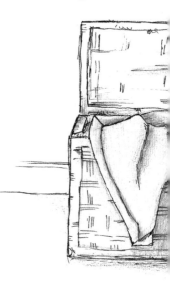

the silky edge of the blanket. Her love for her blankie and her hatred for the Bad Thing and the Bad Person overwhelmed her at the same time, so she quickly drew her hand back and curled up on the floor, crying softly, her belly aching with those feelings. As time went by and her tears came more slowly, she drew herself to her knees and dug out the blanket carefully. She held it in her hands and looked at it as though examining it before wiping

her wet face on the soft pink flannel. Quietly, reverently, she folded it and placed it back at the bottom of her toy box. The lid closed without making a sound, and she made her way back to her bed. It took her a long time to fall asleep.

Mara

Something awakened Gracie late in the night. Was it a sound? Soft and low, like a moan from far away? It was quiet now, and she wasn't sure she had even heard anything. She opened her eyes, and they grew wide and unbelieving as she made out the shape of a door in the wall where no door was supposed to be.

Gracie sat straight up, her heart pounding wildly and her breaths coming quick and short. She jerked her head around to look for Nicholas and sighed with relief as she saw him there, safe and sound, sleeping in his little bed.

S he must look more closely at the Door. "No sense just sitting here being afraid," she reasoned. One leg at a time, forcing herself to keep breathing normally, Gracie pulled herself out of bed and tiptoed across the room.

I n all ways, the Door looked just like any other normal door. A soft light, nothing like sunlight but not an eerie light, either, glowed under and around the edges. The knob matched her bedroom door exactly. It did not seem any newer than anything else in their apartment, and it was painted the same color as all of the doors and the window facings, so it did not seem scary at all for Gracie to reach out and touch the knob.

It did not feel cold, even though it was made from metal just like her other doorknobs. In fact, its warmth was inviting enough for Gracie to decide it was probably safe to turn it. Almost as though the thought of turning it was enough, the Door silently opened and Gracie was on the other side.

She was in a sort of dreary kind of garden, the kind of garden that has been neglected for quite a while so that nothing seems well cared for, and the vines had grown over the statues, and the trees seemed too big, and there were no flowers, but there were plenty of boxwood shrubs. Gracie could smell them, too, and she did not like the smell of boxwoods particularly. The sky was covered in a thick layer of grey clouds so that even the very idea of a sun seemed like a ridiculous notion. The too-big trees were of a sort whose leaves were on long flowing branches that reached toward the ground rather than upward to the unseen sun.

For all this, Gracie was not afraid. There was grass under her feet, and she could hear water nearby, not a flowing river sound, but the sound of a lake or pond whose waters were lapping softly at the shore. She made up her mind to follow this watery sound, and as soon as she decided, a path was in front of her that seemed to invite her to join it.

She walked along the little path through trees and vine-covered statues (everything was surrounded by those boxwoods) until rounding a curve, she saw that the trees were growing

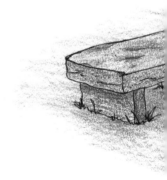

closer together here. Even through the thickly draping branches of the trees, she could catch glimpses of water. On the other side of the trees, the shoreline was covered with thick clumps of overgrown grass. A stone bench stood close to the water, and on the stone bench sat a lady whose pink satin gown appeared to have seen better days. Gracie could not yet see the lady's face. She was lost in thought, looking toward the murky green waters of the lake. Not wanting to interrupt the silence, Gracie studied the shoreline. The tall grasses waded out into the lake for some distance,

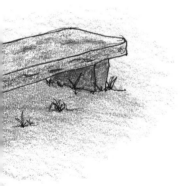

creating a tangle of weeds; but underneath the matted brown growth, Gracie could see the outline of a small boat tethered close to the shore. The lady spoke.

"Hello, Gracie. My name is Mara. Finally, you have come to visit me."

Not knowing what to make of this, Gracie could not reply.

"You are wondering how I know you. Well, I have always known you. I hope we shall be great friends, you and I."

"There was a Door in my room… I just… walked through it…" Gracie stumbled over her words. "What is this place?" she asked as she walked nearer to where the lady sat.

The lady's eyes were blue, like Gracie's, and her hair was brown, a shade or two darker than Gracie's own. Her face was tired and sad, and the dress she

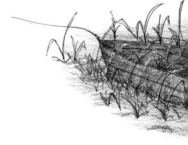

wore seemed as though it would never look really fresh and clean, no matter how many times it was put into the washing machine. Next to her on the stone bench was a large cloth bag of some sort, also dingy pink, and it made Gracie think of her own blanket tucked away in her toybox in her room at home. Did this lady carry a baby blanket with her? Gracie grinned before she had time to remember that it was rude to laugh at people.

"You have noticed my backpack," the lady said, reaching out a hand to touch the pink fabric gently. "It contains something that I must carry with me always, something that gets heavier with the years. It was given to me against my will, but I cannot let it go."

"Why not?" asked Gracie. "What would happen if you left it at home one day?"

The lady smiled at her as if she were tolerating a silly child. "Oh, that would be impossible, you know. It would make my entire life seem as if it did not matter, as if this Bad Thing had never happened to me. I would be living a lie, and that would be wrong, wouldn't it?"

Gracie thought about this very hard. "If someone gave me something I didn't want, I don't think I would keep it," she finally said, hesitantly. "I would... I don't know... send it someplace far away where I would never have to look at it again."

The lady made a noise and waved her hand in the air as though brushing off Gracie's words. "Well, you are only seven years old, so what do you know about it anyway?"

This seemed a little harsh to Gracie, but it also seemed reasonable, so she decided to talk about something else rather than argue. "Are there other people who live in this place?" she asked the lady, who was now focusing on the murky brown lake again.

"Oh, yes, quite a number, but they are very unpleasant people, and so I mind my own business." At this, she looked down at her dingy pink backpack and sighed. Then she straightened her shoulders and shook her head as if to clear it out so that she could speak again. "Old Mrs. Carson lives across the street from my house, but I don't like her much. She watches TV all day long, just like years ago when she was supposed to be taking care of me and my brother. So I never bother to visit her or talk with her."

Gracie nearly jumped when she heard this. "Mara and her brother stayed with Mrs. Carson, just like Nicky and me?" Gracie thought. Then, looking into Mara's face, so grown up, but so like her own, Gracie began to feel a little sick. Everything was starting to feel very strange. She looked at the waters of the lake, and they began to swirl, right in front of her eyes, the greenish-brown waters mingling with the dead brown grass and the dull pink of the lady's backpack and the grey of the sky… the grey of the sky…

Carissa

ommy was touching her on the shoulder, saying, "Gracie, honey, wake up. It's Saturday. We're going to the Flower Park, remember? Eat your breakfast and get dressed!"

For a few short seconds, Gracie was confused. Where was the lake? And the lady? Drawing in a quick breath, she looked toward The Door. It wasn't there! Was the whole thing a dream? But she'd never had a dream quite so real before.

The Flower Park was one of Gracie's favorite places. Mother would drop Nicky off at a friend's house for the day, and Gracie would have

Mommy all to herself. They liked to see what was blooming and try to decide which flowers were their favorites. Mommy always loved the roses, but no matter how beautiful all of the other flowers were, Gracie could not help but adore the daisies. Especially the white ones with the yellow centers.

They just looked so happy and cheerful as if nothing in the world could make them sad. "I can't be sad when I look at them," she announced to her mother each time they visited the park. And there was a whole field full of them today.

After their day at the park, they went to the coffee shop where they tasted cookies from the plate on top of the display case.

Mommy drank coffee while Gracie sipped fruit juice and enjoyed the smells and sights of the place. Grocery shopping was next, then they picked up Nicky and went home to nap for awhile. Saturday evenings were usually full of games, pizza, and popcorn. Gracie loved Saturdays with Mommy. Falling asleep was easy after such a happy day!

Sometime in the night, Gracie found herself awake and staring hard at a Door across the room where no door should be. She blinked and looked again, but it was still there. It was exactly the same as the Door she went through last night, but she wasn't sure she wanted to meet Mara again.

The light seeping around the edges of the Door was welcoming, even though it was not very bright. It beckoned her, and something deep inside Gracie made her want to follow this adventure, too. She slid out of bed and reached for the knob, but the Door was already opening silently into a lovely garden. The sun shone high above, not too hot, but warming her skin and the very roots of her hair. There weren't any boxwoods, but Gracie noticed well-kept pink rose bushes and large clumps of yellow-faced daisies everywhere. There were some trees of a sort that made Gracie want to climb them and sit in their branches, which were just right for a little girl to dream in.

She had been making her way down a path

as she admired the flowers and trees, and the path rounded a curve so that Gracie could now see a beautiful blue lake spread out before her as far as she could see to where a peninsula jutted out to her right and the lake disappeared around it. The shore of the lake was covered in new-mown green grass that made Gracie glad she was not wearing any shoes. There was a little brown boat tethered to a dock, and since the dock was surrounded by what seemed like a very sturdy railing, Gracie wanted very much to walk out onto it, so she could look down into the water. And so that is exactly what she did.

Gracie was busy looking at the reflection of the clouds and the blue sky in the clear water when she heard a musical voice exclaim, "Why, hello, Gracie! I am so glad you have come!"

Gracie turned to see a beautiful lady approaching across the grass at the shore. Her white cotton dress was belted by a pink satin sash at her waist, exactly the same shade of pink as the ribbon on her straw hat. Barefooted like Gracie, she seemed to float rather than walk, and Gracie thought that this lady must be a dancer. Or a gardener, she corrected, for the lady held a huge bundle of freshly cut daisies in her arms, which she deposited on a stone bench before running up the dock to give Gracie a hug. Then she held her away from her by the shoulders and looked at her intently while saying, "Why, Gracie, you are so lovely and so grown up! Oh, silly me! Look at you, you are so wide-eyed, and I hope you are not afraid of me. My name is Carissa, and I brought you some daisies. I hope you like them!"

"I like daisies," Gracie managed to say with some difficulty, although she really liked this lady and how safe she had felt when she was being hugged. The lady smelled of sunshine and clean water and all of the best outdoorsy smells.

"Yes, of course you do," the lady said, and laughed a musical little trill. "Don't you love it here? So much fresh air and sunshine and water. And of course daisies! And so many nice people, too. There's old Mrs. Carson… I always take her a bouquet of daisies. You don't mind if we give her some of these, do you? I knew you wouldn't." Carissa looked at Gracie for a long moment

before asking, "So what brings you here today, Gracie?"

"There was a Door… a strange Door. It was there last night, too. I sort of wanted to go through it again, but I thought… someone else might be here…" Gracie trailed off.

"Oh, you have met Mara, then?" Carissa looked thoughtful and studied Gracie carefully. Gracie nodded, and Carissa took a deep breath before she spoke. "Mara sees this world very differently than I do, and so that is what you saw. A world that is dreary and sad, although she could change it if she would."

Gracie considered this for a moment, and, suddenly, the Bad Thing came into her

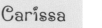

mind. She pushed it away quickly. She was afraid of what Carissa would think if she knew.

"Did Mara show you her backpack?" Carissa asked. When Gracie nodded, Carissa reached into her pocket and brought out a small, dingy pink satin pouch. To Gracie, it looked like a coin purse that her great-grandmother had in her attic. Carissa put it in Gracie's hand, and it fit perfectly into the hollow of her palm.

"Gracie, the three of us were all treated the same way when we were little. Mara feels she must hold onto the memory of the Bad Thing. She thinks that if she does not keep remembering it, she is not living an honest life. Perhaps she feels that she is in some way punishing the Bad Person for doing the Bad Thing." Carissa sighed softly, shaking her head. Then she straightened and took Gracie's hand. She led her off the dock and to the grassy shore where the boat was bobbing gently in the water close by.

"Did you notice the boat in the lake when you were last here, Gracie?"

"Yes, but it was hard to see because it was under the weeds," she answered.

"This is our Send-Away Boat, Gracie. Whenever I feel the weight of the bad memory, I put it into this little boat, and I give it a tremendous push, sending it out into the lake. The current

then takes it away, past the dock and around the peninsula, so that I cannot see it any more. My heart feels light and free. Sometimes, I remember the Bad Thing, or other Bad Things that have happened to me along the way, and still there is the Send-Away Boat, always ready to accept what I cannot hold." Carissa's eyes clouded a little as she continued, "For I have seen what happens when I refuse to send away."

As the lady was saying this, Gracie was studying the little purse in her hand. "If I don't … send it away…" Gracie paused, afraid to ask the question. But Carissa was encouraging her with her kind blue eyes (so much like mine, Gracie thought), so

Gracie continued. "Will it get heavy and big, like Mara's backpack?"

Carissa's eyes were moist, but she smiled as she nodded. "Yes, Mara's back is quite bent from carrying that load, and I fear her heart is bent as well. But I am hoping for better things for you, dear Gracie!"

Gracie held the purse over the Send-Away Boat and looked at Carissa with an unspoken question on her face. Carissa nodded and said, "Yes, Gracie. You can send that away. I do not want it. Neither do you."

And Gracie dropped it in.

Together they pushed the little boat as hard as they could, laughing a lot when they lost their balance and fell into the water. The lady helped Gracie up, then lifted her into her arms and walked onto the dock where they could watch the boat travel around the peninsula. Gracie's heart felt light as a feather, more full of joy than she had ever felt, and she wrapped her arms around Carissa's neck and laid her cheek against hers.

Then it was morning, and Mommy was laying her hand on Gracie's cheek. Gracie's eyes fluttered open, and she smiled into her mother's eyes. Sleepily (and probably not very coherently), Gracie told her about Mara and Carissa. She kept talking even when her mother gathered Gracie into her arms on her lap. She kept talking even when she felt her mother's warm tears on the top of her head.

And after the story was over, Gracie put her hands on each side of her mother's face, looked into her mother's eyes and said, "And Mommy, you know what the best part is? The Send-Away Boat always comes back empty, and it's always there, and we can put anything we want inside of it and push it into the lake. And that makes us feel better so that we want to give people daisies!"

The End

A Note for Parents

The Send-Away Boat is intended as a metaphor for forgiveness, a concept that most children – not to mention adults – have difficulty with. In the characters of Mara (from the Hebrew word meaning *"bitter"*) and Carissa (adapted from the Greek word charis, meaning *"grace"*), children are given a stark contrast between the results of the choice to forgive or not to forgive an offense. In this story, Gracie receives a rare opportunity to meet her future self, the self she will become over the years as she daily makes her choice. Perhaps this contrast will facilitate the right choice and empower children to live life free from the crippling effects of lingering emotional pain.

*W*here Jesus discussed the need to forgive, the Gospels use a Greek word meaning, literally, *"to send away."* Somehow, this concept seems more easily embraced and employed than its English equivalent. This story also addresses the reality of recurring memories and the necessity of repeated forgiveness (sending away) in a nonjudgmental way. It is important to remind your child that the fact that the sending away needs to be redone does not imply that the forgiveness was not real in the first place. Can we not re-forgive the same offense as needed?

*T*he simplicity of this story is not intended to trivialize any particular offense against children; rather, it is intended to provide a strong internal pattern of sending away offenses as soon as they occur, and as often as necessary, giving our children a powerful tool that can benefit them all of their lives. It is our prayer that this story will become fixed in your child's imagination, and in yours as well, as all of us deal with the offenses that come our way. While it is true that we cannot change the unloving and often tragic things that happen to us at the hands of other people, we must ourselves choose whether to send away the offense or not, and in that choice lies a great and awesome power.

My Notes:

Shelly Forgey is a wife, mother, grandmother, Bible Study leader, and former home school mom who has also been a college math teacher, math education consultant, church worship leader, musician, singer, and actress in community theater productions. She also loves to sew, quilt, and garden. Her interest in sending away offenses arises from two contexts: her personal experiences in that area, and her experiences as a volunteer counselor working with women in crisis centers. She has three grown children and three grandchildren. She and her husband Steve have been married for thirty years, and they live in Cookeville, Tennessee, with their dog Molly. It is her hope that the Gracie Books will give children strong internal patterns for dealing with pain from offenses so that they can live emotionally free and happy lives.

True Potential, Inc
PO Box 904
Travelers Rest, SC 29690
www.truepotentialmedia.com

True Potential
REACH THE WORLD